P9-CQJ-662
3 9082 08829 1219

A gift from
THE
BROWNSTONE
BOOK FUND

BURT DOW
DEEP-WATER MAN

Also by Robert McCloskey

LENTIL
MAKE WAY FOR DUCKLINGS
HOMER PRICE
BLUEBERRIES FOR SAL
CENTERBURG TALES
ONE MORNING IN MAINE
TIME OF WONDER

TURPS

BURT DOW
DEEP-WATER MAN

A TALE OF THE
SEA IN THE
CLASSIC
TRADITION

BY ROBERT McCLOSKEY

THE VIKING PRESS, NEW YORK

VIKING
Published by the Penguin Group
Viking Penguin, a division of Penguin Books
USA Inc., 345 Hudson Street, New York,
New York 10014, U.S.A.
Penguin Books Ltd, 27 Wrights Lane,
London W8 5TZ, England
Penguin Books Australia Ltd, Ringwood,
Victoria, Australia
Penguin Books Canada Ltd,
Penguin Books (N.Z.) Ltd, 182–190 Wairau
Road, Auckland 10, New Zealand

Penguin Books Ltd, Registered Offices:
Harmondsworth, Middlesex, England

First published in 1963 by The Viking Press, Inc.

Library of Congress catalog card number 62-15446
ISBN 0-670-19748-3

20 19 18

Manufactured in China

BURT DOW

DEEP-WATER MAN

Burt Dow is an old deep-water man, retired of course, but retired or not he still keeps two boats. One is a dory so old and so leaky that it can no longer be launched. Burt has painted it red and placed it on the little patch of lawn in front of his house, overlooking the bay.

He's rigged it like one of the many ships he's sailed to all the

corners of all the seven seas. It's filled plumb to the gun'ls with earth, and every summer Burt plants it with geraniums and Indian peas. The geraniums brighten up the deck, and the Indian peas climb the rigging and sway this-a-way, that-a-way, in a smoky sou'wester.

The other boat is an old double-ender named *Tidely-Idley,* with a make-and-break engine. This boat leaks too, except when it's pulled up on shore for caulking, patching, and painting, which is most of the time.

"She's a good boat," says Burt, patting her on the stern and giving her propeller an affectionate kick. "She's got a few tender places in her planking, but you can't see daylight through her nowheres."

The *Tidely-Idley* is the pride and joy of Burt's life, and between odd jobs for natives and summer people he keeps her painted and patched as best he can. Every time he does a paint job, he brings home the leftover paint and uses it on the *Tidely-Idley*.

"That pink plank," he says, "is the color of Ginny Poor's pantry ...and the green one is the color of the floor and doors in Doc Walton's waiting-room...and there's the tan porch and trim color from Capt'n Haskell's house."

Burt Dow has a sister named Leela who keeps house for him, cooks the lobsters and fish he catches and the clams he digs. She feeds the cock, she feeds the hens, she tends the garden, and she helps Burt keep down the weeds in the dory full of geraniums and Indian peas.

Leela is a very impatient person—"Most impatient being on land or sea," says Burt, and he hustles about doing this or that so as not to keep her waiting.

Mornings, when the cock crows, "Cockety-doodly," Leela is already down in the kitchen rattling her stove lids, klinkety-klink, and shouting, "Hit the deck, Burt! Time to eat!" And Burt, winking and blinking his eyelids, comes stumbling down the stairs to breakfast so as not to keep Leela waiting.

Burt Dow has a giggling gull for a pet. Every morning she roosts on the roof of the shed where Burt keeps his fishing gear.

The gull giggles, "Tee-he-he-hee!" until Burt comes out and tosses her a pancake or a popover, or sometimes a piece of cinnamon toast.

When Burt Dow puts out to sea in the *Tidely-Idley,* everybody in town knows it. They hear him pump out all the water that has leaked in overnight, slish-cashlosh, slish-cashlosh! Then there is a pause while Burt checks the tenderest spot—between the pink plank (the color of

Ginny Poor's pantry) and the green plank (the color of the floor and doors in Doc Walton's waiting-room).

Then they hear him start the make-and-break engine, clackety *bang!* clackety *bang!* And they see him, firm hand on the tiller, giggling gull flying along behind, heading out of the cove and going clackety-bangety down the bay.

One morning the cock crowed, "Cockety-doodly," and Leela rattled her stove lids klinkety-klink, shouting, "Hit the deck, Burt, time to eat!" And Burt came downstairs winking and blinking his sleepy eyelids and ate his breakfast.

He tossed the giggling gull a popover—"Tee-he-he-hee!"—and went down to the cove to pump out the *Tidely-Idley,* slish-cashlosh, slish-cashlosh.

He gently felt the tender spot between the pink plank (the color of Ginny Poor's pantry) and the green plank (the color of the floor and doors in Doc Walton's waiting-room).

"Giggling gull," he said sadly, "'twon't be long before the *Tidely-Idley* gets planted with geraniums and Indian peas."

Then he started the make-and-break, clackety-BANG! clackety-BANG! And, firm hand on the tiller, giggling gull flying along behind, he headed out of the cove, going clackety-bangety down the bay to fish for cod.

Burt kept studying the color of the sky, the color of the water, and the direction of the wind.

"An old deep-water man like me always keeps a weather eye out," says Burt, "but he keeps *two* weather eyes out when he puts out to sea in a vessel as old and leaky as the *Tidely-Idley!*"

It looked like a good day, so Burt took the *Tidely-Idley* way, way out to the end of the bay and into the open sea. He shut off the make-and-break engine and let the boat drift on the gentle swell. Then he baited up his hook with clams and lowered it over the side to fish for cod.

Burt didn't get any bites, not even a teeny-weeny nibble, so he cranked up the make-and-break and moved the *Tidely-Idley* to another spot.

But there were no fish there either. He didn't even pull up a pollock or a sculpin.

"There must be something down there frightening those fish!" Burt confided to the giggling gull.

"Tee-he-he-hee!" the giggling gull agreed.

Then Burt felt a substantial sort of tug on his line that almost, but not quite, pulled him over the side.

Then Burt pulled...and then Burt tugged...he heaved and he tugged, he grunted and groaned until the *Tidely-Idley* practically stood on end.

But he couldn't haul in even a single stitch of line.

"Must be caught on the bottom," said Burt.

"Tee-he-he-hee!" The giggling gull was much amused and she teetered on the tip of the tiller to see what would happen next.

Well, Burt, so it seemed, finally got his line uncaught from the bottom and was hauling it in, in a moderate sort of way, not paying much attention, to see if he needed more bait.

The giggling gull was teetering to and fro on the tip of the tiller and tittering "Tee-he-he-hee!" now and then, in a nervous sort of way.

She might have noticed something or other that for that particular moment hadn't come to Burt's attention.

But the very *next* moment it came to Burt's attention that he'd pulled up a

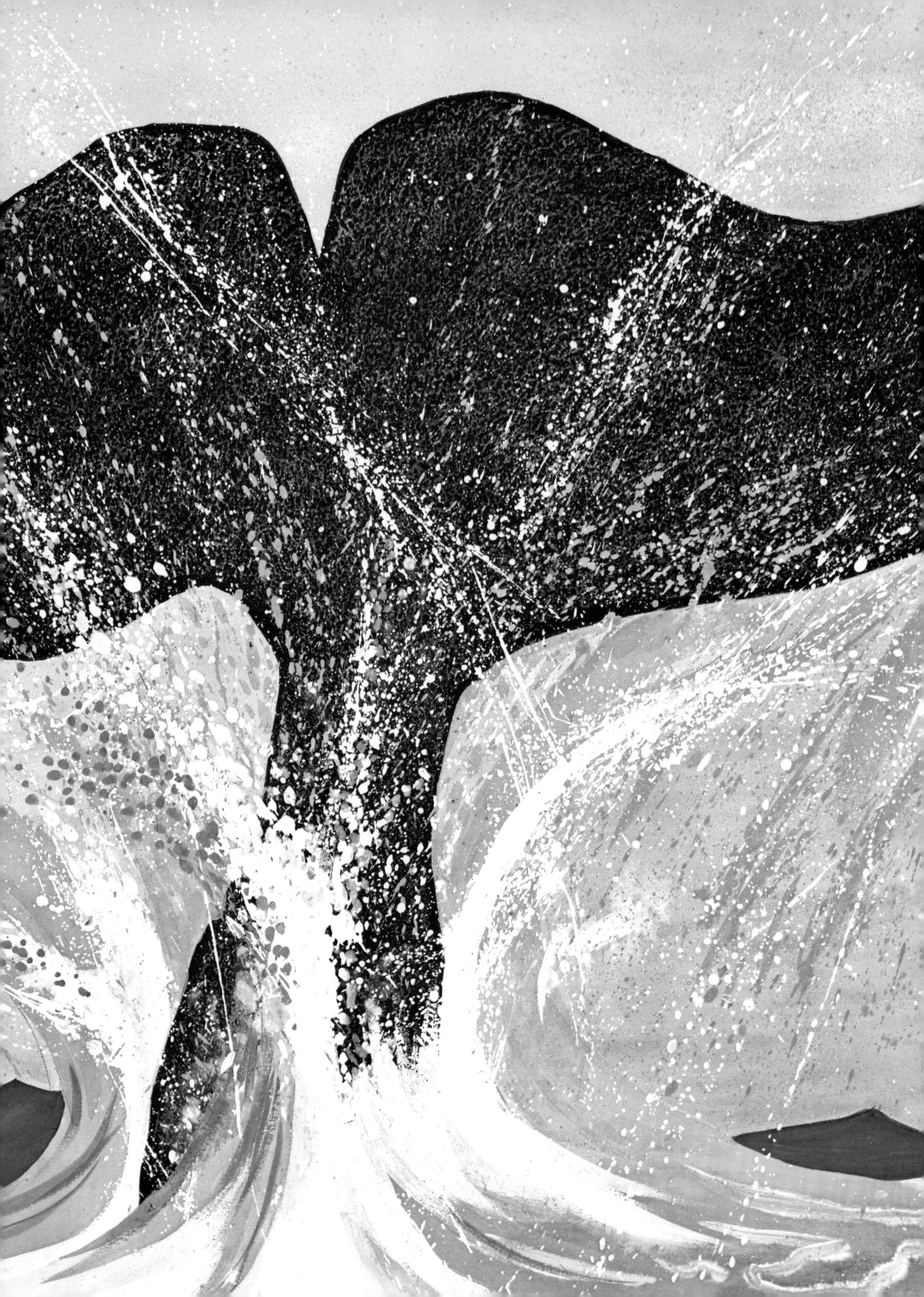

WHALE OF A TAIL!...

Or 'twas t'other-way-round — the tail of a whale had pulled up *Burt!*

Burt grabbed the pump handle and hung on while he swung around, this-a-way, that-a-way. The giggling gull teetered on the tip of the tiller and laughed fit to split.

Burt finally slacked up on the line, or 'twas t'other-way-round — finally the *tail* slacked up on the line. But then the tail began to thrash about, this-a-way, that-a-way, in such a manner as to call Burt's attention to the fact that there was a

whale on the other end of it.

"Ahoy there, whale!" bellowed Burt. "Hold your horses! Keep your shirt on! Head into the wind and slack off the main sheet!"

The whale couldn't hear because his hearing gear was so far upwind from his steering gear that had come afoul of Burt's cod hook.

"Ahoy there, you giggling gull!" shouted Burt. "Fly away down there and tell this whale that this vessel has a couple of tender places in her planking. He's about to stave us in and send the *Tidely-Idley* and all hands straight to Davy Jones's locker!"

The barb of Burt's cod hook was barely caught in the blubber of the tail, and since it didn't hurt, the whale quieted down and allowed Burt to haul in his cod line cautiously, so he could remove the hook.

When the tail came within reach, Burt had his pliers ready. Working ever so carefully so as not to tickle, he snipped off the barb and eased out the hook.

"There, now!" said Burt. "Only a little bit of a hole, and I've got just the thing for that."

He reached down in the bottom of his tool kit and brought out a box of band-aids Doc Walton had given him (just in case a lobster ever took a nip out of a finger). They were decorated with peppermint stripes, and fortunately they were the kind that

stick to *anything*, even *whale tails!*

"There, now, Cap'n Whale!" said Burt proudly. "I'll wager your rudder won't leak out any blubber or take aboard any water and get waterlogged now."

But just then—CA-SMACK! A whopping big wave caught the *Tidely-Idley* in a very embarrassing position and jolted her to the bottom of her keel, all the way from prow to propeller!

Burt had forgotten to keep his weather eyes out, what with getting this poor whale out of all the trouble he was in, and hadn't noticed that it was beginning to blow. ("Tip of his tail snagged on a cod hook—all his blubber 'bout to dribble through the hole!...")

Burt started the make-and-break engine and managed to head the *Tidely-Idley* into the wind, but he knew he'd never make it home. However, he did make it to the leeward side of the whale and, with a firm hand on the tiller, giggling gull flying along behind, headed chuggety-bangety up to the bow of the whale to have a face-to-face talk.

"It's blowin' a gale of wind, whale!" bellowed Burt, coming right to the point. "And one good turn deserves another.

"The *Tidely-Idley's* taking aboard water between those two tender planks. I'm a-pumping just as fast as I can pump, but the water's above the floor boards and 'bout to stall the make-and-break. I'm afeared this vessel and all hands aboard are headed for Davy Jones's locker!

"No doubt the *Tidely-Idley*'d taste terrible," Burt went on, still coming right to the point, "and her barnacled bottom would smart your tongue, whale. The make-and-break would taste bitter as bile, and me, an old deep-water man in oilskins and boots, 'long with this giggling gull, would make gosh-awful trimmings for any meal—*but,*" pleaded Burt, "couldn't you just sort of *swallow* us—temporary, of course—while this gale of wind blows itself out?"

The whale gave a little snort and didn't say anything. Apparently this was a whale of few words. He just

opened his mouth wide and said, "AH-H-H!"—in the classic tradition.

Burt set the throttle of the make-and-break at wide open and, chuggeta-bang! chuggeta-bang! firm hand on the tiller, giggling gull flying along behind, guided the *Tidely-Idley* into the whale's mouth and navigated the length of the gullet and into the whale's tummy, without so much as touching a tonsil on the way down!

"Well!" said Burt. "I naturally expected it to be dark inside a whale's tummy, but I didn't expect it to be as dark as this. A few portholes for light and ventilation would improve the design of this animal."

This idea struck the giggling gull as funny, and she started giggling again. Burt was bending over and bumbling about in the dark, trying to find his lantern. He bumped his head on the make-and-break and yelled, "Out of my way, you chuggety, bangafied batch of old iron!"

"Tee-he-he-hee!" This made the giggling gull laugh fit to split.

"Gull," Burt said testily, "some day I'll *gaggle* you! I never realized until now how limited your vocabulary is. You'd be a poor companion to be shipwrecked on a sunny desert island with, and you're even worse in dry dock, down in this dark, damp tummy of a whale. If I had my choice, I'd take a dictionary every time."

Burt had found the lantern and was feeling around, trying to find a dry spot on which to strike a match, when he had a very disquieting thought.

"Supposing this whale didn't hear every word I said out there in that gale of wind?" he asked. "What if he doesn't understand the English language red-letter perfect? Or maybe that he's absent-minded? He might not know, or remember, that we're supposed to be *temporary* guests, so to speak.

"Yup, giggling gull," Burt continued, "we'll have to make sure we get ourselves *unswallowed!"*

He finally struck a match (used the seat of his pants).

"Well!" he said as the light flared up. "I naturally expected *pink* would be the color of this whale's tummy, but I wasn't prepared for pink *identical* with the pink in Ginny Poor's pantry! Yup! Like a big pink cave, that's what it is."

Burt checked over his boat and found that the spot where the wave had slapped the *Tidely-Idley* on her tender bottom would need considerable caulking, patching, and painting. In fact, the water that only moments before had leaked from the ocean *into* the *Tidely-Idley*

was now leaking t'other-way-round, *out* of the *Tidely-Idley* and on to the pink deck of the whale's tummy.

After Burt finished his caulking, patching, and painting, he said, "'Tain't perfect, but she'll hold until we get home, I *hope!*

"Giggling gull, we have to get busy! Leela's back home, rattling her stove lids and getting impatient over our not being home in time to eat!"

First of all, Burt tugged and shoved until he got the *Tidely-Idley*

turned about so that her bow pointed in the right direction. *Then* he systematically set about trying to give the whale an upset tummy.

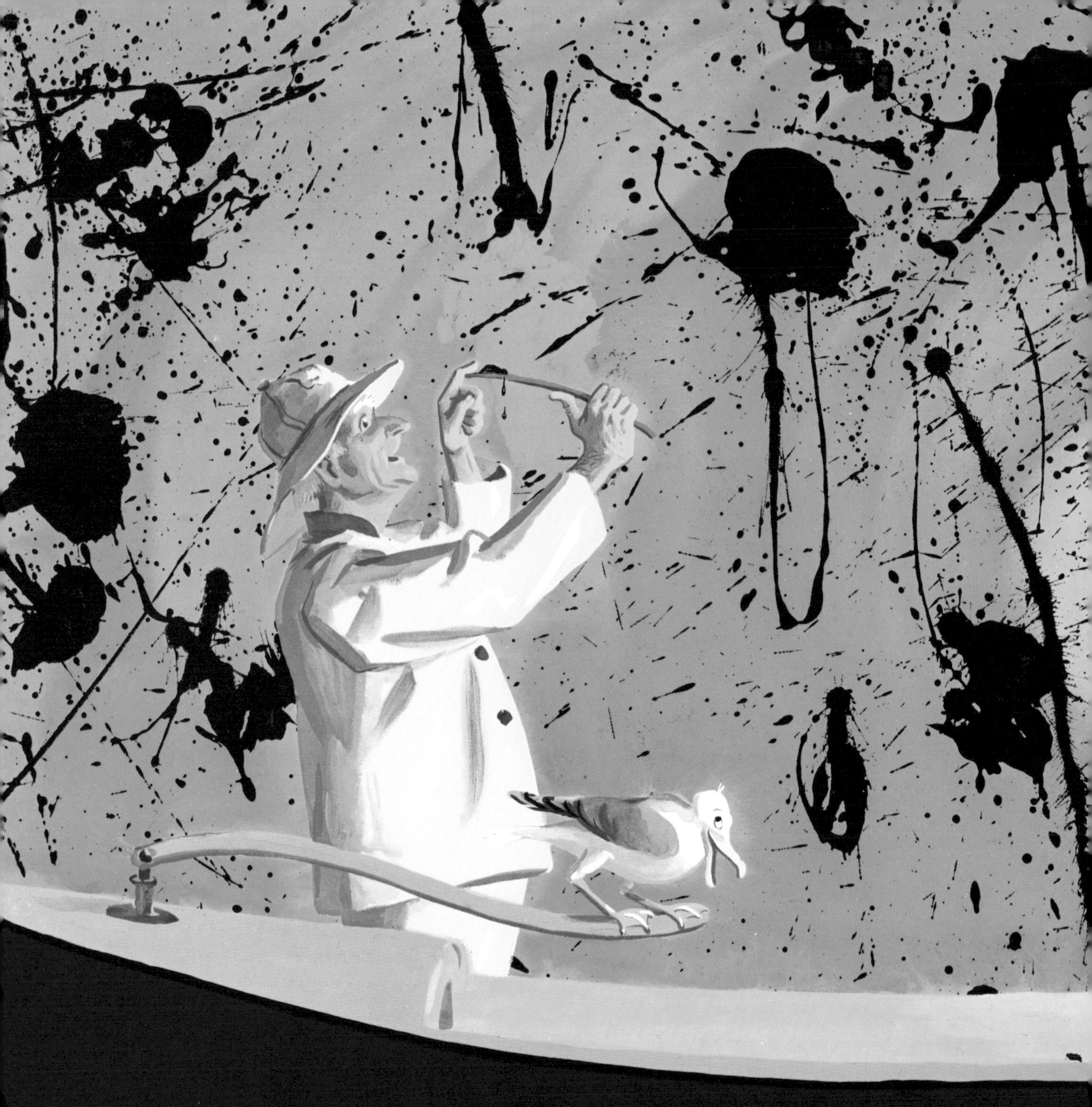

"Whales has got strong stomachs," Burt explained to the giggling gull, "and it takes more than a mixture of catsup and ice cream, pickles and peppermint, mince pie and mustard, to call their attention to the fact that their tummy's upset."

He began by pumping out the *Tidely-Idley* to the very bottom of

the bilge. In an old boat, that always produces a lot of interesting things, such as old crab claws, clams, bait, rusty fishhooks, a can opener, corroded pieces of brass, all mixed in with a nice big helping of *sediment*. Burt started scooping up the sediment on the end of a piece of shingle and began flipping a-little-gob-here, a-little-gob-there, making big splatter spots on the lining of the tummy. The tummy began to quiver like

a horse's flanks flicking off flies!

Then Burt opened a left-over gallon of yellow deck paint and started sloshing it around, dribbling a-little-bit-here, a-little-bit-there. He was beginning to enjoy himself—probably because it was the first time he'd ever had a chance really to express his personality in paint.

Next he took a can of cup grease and, with the shingle, started spattering a few accents here and there.

By now the whale's tummy was *all* a-quiver! It disturbed Burt's aim a bit, and he misplaced a few blobs of cup grease. Well! The tummy began

to make rumbling noises and flip-a-lot this-a-way, flip-a-lot that-a-way, and Burt knew right off that it would take only the littlest touch to make the tummy break loose from its moorings and get upset.

He, quick as he could, jumped into the *Tidely-Idley* and started the

"Giggling gull!" he shouted. "Wiggle your wings and fly away up into the for'ard hatchway and tickle this whale's throat with a feather!"

Of course the exhaust and jiggling of the make-and-break helped, but 'twas the tickle that turned the trick! With the dark dampest rumble ever heard, the big tummy flipped this-a-way, that-a-way, and

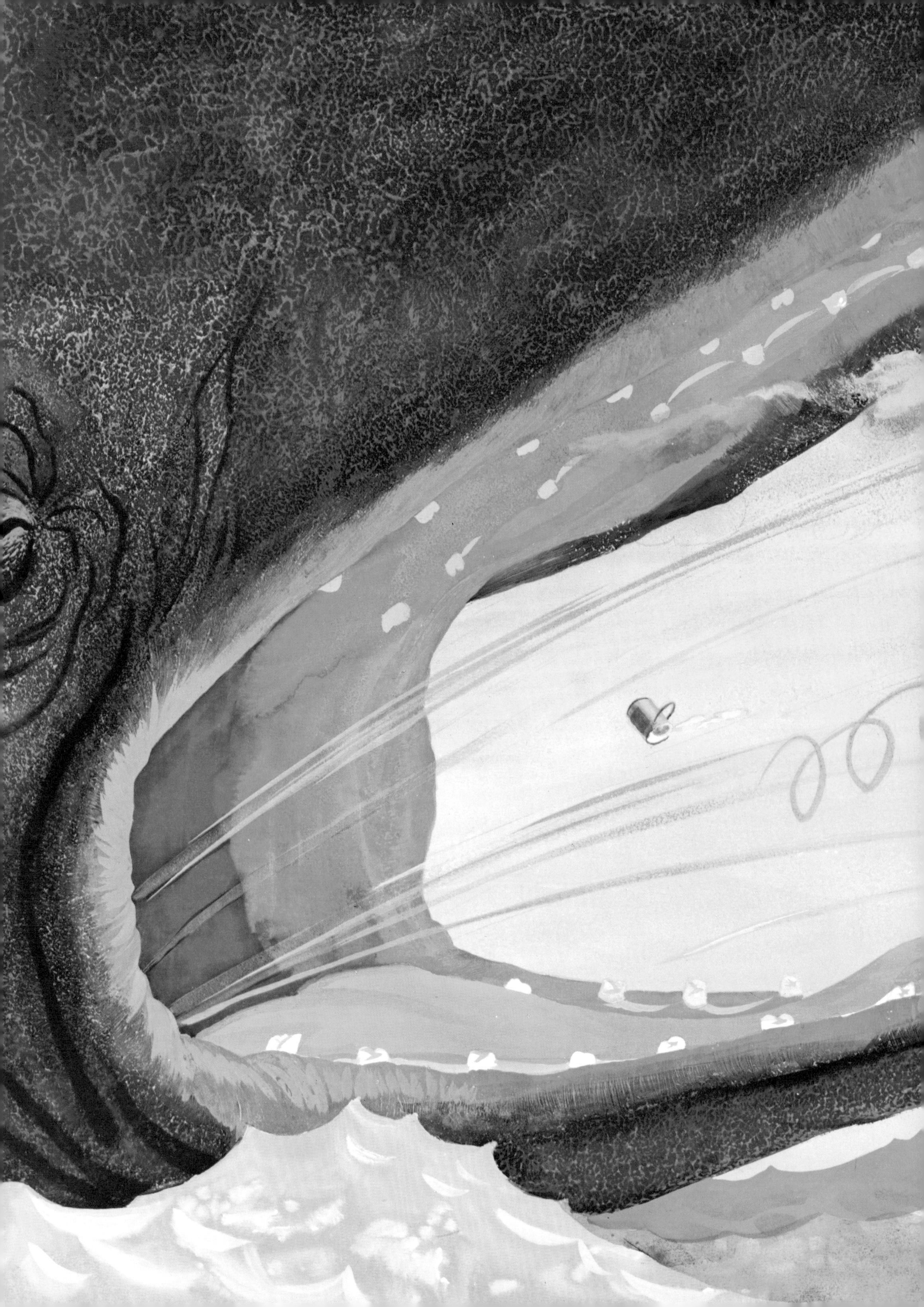

with a whale of a "BURP!" boat and Burt, firm hand on the tiller, giggling gull flying along behind, make-and-break going wide open, came clackety-bangety out of the wide open mouth of the whale, going so fast that they barely touched the tops of the first two waves and landed right dab

SMACK! in the middle of a whole school of whales! Burt eased up on the throttle of the make-and-break and tried to steer a snug course between two whale-tails, one the color of Ginny Poor's pantry, t'other the color of the floor and doors in Doc Walton's waiting-room, but the way was blocked by a whale-tail the color of the porch and trim on Cap'n Haskell's house. Every time Burt shifted course, there seemed to be more whale-tails in the way. Finally Burt stopped the make-and-

break and let the *Tidely-Idley* drift among the whale-tails while he decided what to do next.

He bobbed around in his boat, studying the situation. Then he took out his glass and studied some more. Then he finally said, "Well!!! That's a whale of a lot of whale-tails"—making what amounted to a classic understatement. "You can hardly see the forest for the trees," Burt complained, "or the whales for the tails!"

There must be some reason, thought Burt, why all this school of whales are waving their tails toward the *Tidely-Idley*.

"All except one," he added, peeping through his glass at a pale whale that looked exactly as though it had an upset tummy from a bit of bilge-water, cup grease, deck paint, and having its throat tickled by a feather. "Yup! That whale looks a bit under the weather, but it also looks *contented*."

But meanwhile the rest of the school of whales seemed to be getting impatient. They twitched the tips of their tails and *whacked* them down on the water.

"Careful!" bellowed Burt. "The *Tidely-Idley's* got a tender spot, and you're apt to spring a seam—if first you don't swat us like a fly, which is no fit way for an old deep-water man and his vessel to go to Davy Jones."

What with the *Tidely-Idley's* regular leaks, and all the water being splashed aboard by impatient whale-tails, Burt had to keep pumping, slish-cashlosh, slish-cashlosh, and he didn't have much time to wonder what made one whale contented and what made all the rest of the school so slap-happy with their tails. Stronger and younger men might have given up, but not our deep-water man, Burt Dow! He kept right on pumping with one hand, slish-cashlosh, slish-cashlosh, while he poked around in his tool box with the other. Still pumping, slish-cashlosh, slish-cashlosh, he pulled out a band-aid, unfurled it from its wrappings between his teeth, and slapped it onto the tip of the nearest whale-tail.

Burt knew right off that his troubles were over.

"The whales were only impatient at my taking so long to understand 'em," Burt explained to the giggling gull. "Whales is really very patient about standing or swimming in line to have the tips of their tails decked out with a band-aid."

After all the whale-tails had been decorated, each with a peppermint-striped band-aid, the entire school swam, tails held high, in a tremendous circle around the *Tidely-Idley*.

An old deep-water man like Burt couldn't resist shouting, "Thar she blows!" in the best classic tradition.

Then all together, *one, two, three,* the school of whales blew three big blows for Burt Dow and swam off over the horizon.

"I never did see," said Burt, "so many tons of contentment come from out of such a little old band-aid box!"

He still had one band-aid left, and he knew he'd never need it himself—never was a lobster hatched or catched as could ever clamp a claw on Burt Dow—so just for a joke he said, "Giggling gull, let's take this last band-aid home to Leela!"

"Tee-he-he-hee!" giggled the gull, because she always was one who enjoyed Burt's little jokes.

"And we'd better take it right now," said Burt, "so's not to keep her waiting."

But then he noticed that

the water was up over the floor boards. So he started pumping again, slish-cashlosh, slish-cashlosh! Then he cranked the make-and-break, clackety-BANG! clackety-BANG! and with a firm hand on the tiller, giggling gull flying along behind, he headed the *Tidely-Idley* back up the bay.

They made it home just as the cock began to crow.

Robert McCloskey (1914-2003) wrote and illustrated some of the most honored and enduring children's books ever published, including *Blueberries for Sal, One Morning in Maine,* and *Homer Price.* He was the first artist to win the Caldecott Medal twice, for *Make Way for Ducklings* in 1942 and *Time of Wonder* in 1958.

His boyhood was spent in Hamilton, Ohio, and he attended the Vesper George School of Art in Boston. For most of his adult life, McCloskey lived in Maine, where he and his wife Peggy raised their two daughters, Sally and Jane. In 2000 Robert McCloskey was named a Living Legend by the Library of Congress.